A Very Strange Place

By

Hilary Mac Austin

Illustrated by

Shawna J. C. Tenney

Mc Graw Hill SR

Columbus, OH

SRAonline.com

Copyright © 2008 by SRA/McGraw-Hill.

All rights reserved. No part of this publication may be
reproduced or distributed in any form or by any means, or
stored in a database or retrieval system, without the prior
written consent of The McGraw-Hill Companies, Inc.,
including, but not limited to, network storage or
transmission, or broadcast for distance learning.

Send all inquiries to this address:
SRA/McGraw-Hill
4400 Easton Commons
Columbus, OH 43219

Printed in the United States of America.

ISBN: 978-0-07-611275-3
MHID: 0-07-611275-6

3 4 5 6 7 8 9 MAL 13 12 11 10 09 08

The *McGraw·Hill* Companies

Contents

1 ◆ A Terrible Place 1

2 ◆ A Sticky Pink Cloud 5

3 ◆ The Ride 10

4 ◆ Turned Around 15

5 ◆ The Whole World 19

6 ◆ Flying 24

Chapter 1

A Terrible Place

Screams filled the air. People were everywhere. Children were running. The air was full of strange smells. What was this terrible place?

Lata grabbed Grandmother's hand. She looked at Uncle and Aunty. Why had they made her come here?

Then she saw something very strange. It was a train track. But it was way up in the air! The track went up and down big hills. The hills were made of metal and wood. Lata had never seen such a thing. Where did these train tracks go?

*Then Lata saw a train stop on the track. She watched the people sit in the open train cars. They looked happy. The train went up a big hill. Then it started to come down.

The train was going too fast. It could not stop! The people on the train were screaming in fear. And the people on the ground* did not even care! They were laughing and smiling. Why was no one helping the people on the train?

"Someone help them!" Lata yelled. "Stop the train! Stop the train!" She began to cry.

Aunty and Uncle looked up at the train. Then they looked at Lata.

"Oh, Lata," Aunty said. "Shh, it's okay. It's no big deal. It's just a ride. The people are safe. It's okay."

Then Lata saw the people getting off the strange train. They weren't hurt. They weren't even scared anymore. They were laughing and happy!

"That's a roller coaster," Aunty said. "It goes fast, but it's very safe. No one will get hurt."

"It's very fun," Uncle said. "It's the best ride there is. Want to try it?"

Lata shook her head.

Chapter 2

A Sticky Pink Cloud

Aunty kissed Lata's cheek. Grandmother wiped away Lata's tears. But Lata did not feel much better.

Lata and Grandmother used to live in a small town. They had just come to live with Uncle and Aunty. Here, everything was new. Everything was fast. Everything was loud!

Today Uncle had made them come to this scary place with strange trains that went too fast. No, Lata did not feel better. She just wanted to go back to her small town.

She closed her eyes and remembered her old home. *She could feel the hot, dry wind. She could see the small mud houses. She could hear the goats. Their bells rang in the empty air. She could smell the cooking fires. And she could feel the dirt on her bare feet.

"Okay, let's have some fun!" Uncle shouted.

Lata opened her eyes. She was back in this strange place.* Her small town was far, far away.

Uncle clapped his hands together. Then he smiled at Lata.

"No need to be scared," he said. "This place is full of fun, fun, fun— you'll see, Lata."

Lata did not think this place was fun. Grandmother looked worried. But Uncle and Aunty seemed happy. Together they walked around the park.

Soon Uncle stopped in front of a small cart. The man with the cart handed Uncle big pink clouds on paper sticks. What was this?

Uncle gave Lata one of the pink clouds. She didn't know what it was. She held it far away from her body. She touched it with one finger. It was sticky. Then Uncle began to eat the pink cloud! So Lata took a small bite of her sticky cloud.

It was sweet! It tasted like sweet air. Lata took a bigger bite. The sticky pink cloud was good! She took an even bigger bite. A long string of sticky pink cloud stuck to her right cheek. She laughed. Uncle and Aunty laughed. Grandmother smiled. Maybe this place wasn't so terrible.

Chapter 3

The Ride

Lata started to feel better. She looked around. Aunty whispered something to Uncle. Then Uncle nodded.

"Come on, Lata. I'm going to show you something fun," he said. He took Lata's hand and started to run. Lata and Uncle ran through the park. Aunty and Grandmother tried to keep up.

"You will love this!" Uncle said. "I know you will."

Suddenly, Uncle stopped running. Lata looked at the sight in front of her and gasped.

She saw a big tent. Inside the tent were horses and other animals. They were going around and around. They were also going up and down. They were on poles around a big wheel. The animals were painted every color under the sun. They were so pretty! They looked like they were leaping and running. Strange music filled the air. But it was fun, happy music.

Lata and Uncle waited for their turn. Then they ran around the wheel, looking at each animal.

*Lata picked a horse painted red and gold. It looked like it was running a race. Uncle picked a horse painted black and green. It looked like it was leaping into the air. Lata and Uncle got on their horses for the ride.

The horses went around and around. They went up and down. And they went faster and faster.* Lata held onto the pole. She leaned back and laughed. She felt safe. Each time she went around she waved at Aunty and Grandmother. It was fun!

13

Lata wanted to ride again and again. She wanted to ride every animal. Aunty went with her on the next ride. Lata rode a horse painted blue, and Aunty rode a horse painted red.

The next time, Lata rode a tiger. She couldn't believe it. She was riding a tiger! Lata laughed and laughed. She waved at Grandmother. Grandmother waved back and smiled.

—Chapter 4—

Turned Around

"Okay, let's have some *more* fun!" Uncle shouted. He was waving and grinning. Lata got off the tiger.

"I have another ride for you. Oh, you will like this. Yes, you will!" Uncle said. He grabbed Lata's hand. Then he started running again.

Soon Lata and Uncle stopped at the new ride. Lata looked. Then she looked again.

She saw big yellow cups. They looked like the cups Aunty used for tea. And people were sitting in the big cups. How strange!

*Lata didn't think this ride would be fun. Sitting in a cup looked silly. But she didn't say anything. Uncle pulled Lata into one of the big cups, and they sat down.

"Oh, you will like this very much," he said. Suddenly, all the cups started moving. What was happening?

The cups were moving in a big circle. It was* just like the tiger ride! Lata laughed. She waved at Aunty and Grandmother.

Just then, her cup started to turn all by itself. Lata grabbed onto the side of the cup. It turned faster and faster. She couldn't see anything clearly. Everything was mixed together. The world was going by so fast!

Lata was going so fast that it was hard to move. She held on tight. She felt strange and dizzy.

But it was a good kind of dizzy. Lata felt like laughing. So she did. The laugh jumped out of her, loud and happy. Once Lata started laughing, she couldn't stop. Soon she and Uncle were laughing and yelling together.

Chapter 5

The Whole World

Lata and Uncle were still laughing when the ride ended. When Lata tried to walk, her legs felt like jelly. She wobbled as she walked. This made her and Uncle laugh even more.

"So you liked that ride?" Uncle asked. Lata nodded.

"Then I have another ride for you. This is a ride we can all do—even Grandmother," Uncle said.

"All right," Aunty said. "But no more running, okay? Let's walk."

"Are you happy?" Grandmother asked Lata.

Lata nodded again and took Grandmother's hand.

Then Lata saw the strangest thing she had ever seen. It was a really, really big wheel. It was turning. And people were sitting in seats on the wheel! They went high into the air. Lata gasped.

"There it is," Uncle said.

Lata felt afraid again. She did not know if she wanted to go on this ride. She looked at Grandmother. Grandmother looked scared too.

"It's okay," Uncle said when he saw their faces. "This is a fun ride."

"It will be safe," Aunty said. "I have been on this ride. I know it is safe. And we will hold on to you."

So Uncle, Aunty, Lata, and Grandmother all got on the big wheel. Uncle and Grandmother sat together. Aunty sat with Lata.

The wheel started to move slowly. The seats in the wheel started to swing a little. Lata grabbed Aunty's hand. She held on tight. Lata could hear Uncle talking to Grandmother. He kept telling her the ride was safe.

Soon Lata got used to the swinging seat. But she was still a little scared. They went higher into the air. Then they went even higher. Soon they were at the top of the big wheel. Lata could see the whole park. The people in the park looked like little ants. She could see the farms around the park too. They looked so green and pretty. Lata forgot to be scared.

"I can see the whole world," she whispered.

"Yes," Aunty said, smiling. "We can see the whole world."

—Chapter 6—

Flying

*Grandmother did not like the big wheel very much. When she got off the ride, she looked a little sick.

"No more flying," she muttered. "I like my feet on the ground."

"That's not flying," Uncle said. "There is another ride where you really fly. Do you want to try it, Lata?"

Flying? It couldn't be. But Lata had never* dreamed she would ride a tiger, or spin in a big cup, or sit at the top of the world!

Flying sounded scary, but it also sounded fun. So Lata slowly nodded her head.

The family walked to the ride. People were flying in seats! The seats were like swings. Lata clapped her hands. There was a swing in her old town. She loved to swing.

But these weren't like any swings Lata had ever seen. The ride was a big pole with a big, flat circle on top. The swings were hanging from the big circle. The circle turned very fast. The swings also turned fast. They swung out and away from the pole. Lata couldn't believe it.

"Oh no," Grandmother said. "No! Lata cannot go on that ride. Those people will fly away! They will fall."

"It's really safe," Uncle said.

Grandmother looked at Aunty. Aunty nodded. Then they all looked at Lata.

"Well, do you want to try it?" Uncle asked her.

"You don't have to. If you are too scared, just tell us," Aunty said.

Grandmother shook her head.

Lata took a deep breath. "Yes!" she said. "Yes, I want to fly on that thing."

So Lata went on the flying ride. She flew in the air, screaming and laughing. She had never had so much fun.

"I love flying," she yelled as she ran back to her family. "I love it!" Uncle gave Lata a big hug.

"Next we'll ride the strange train," he whispered. "Are you ready?"

"Yes!" Lata said, smiling.